ZANE CARRINGTON

SGP
STORMGATE PRESS

stormgatepress.com
stormgatepress@gmail.com

Copyright © 2024 by Charles F. Millhouse
All rights reserved. This book or any portion thereof may not be reproduced or used in any manner whatsoever without the express written permission of the publisher except for the use of brief quotations in a book review or scholarly journal.
First Printing: 2024
ISBN: 9798343717334
Imprint: Independently published

Introducing the Stormgate Press Quick Read Books

Short Story Pulp Adventure Books
Reminiscent of the dime store novels of old.

BOOK 1: The Purple Mystique

BOOK 2: Night Vision

BOOK 3: A Zane Carrington Adventure

BOOK 4: The Purple Mystique: Purple Incognito

BOOK 5: Zane Carrington: The Contract

BOOK 6: Tales From the Other Side of the World: The Barbarian With No Name.

BOOK 7: Zane Carrington: Eternity's Time Clock

BOOK 8: Night Vision: Death Takes a Number (coming soon).

Watch for more books in the series coming soon...

SGP STORMGATE PRESS — MAKING READING FUN AGAIN!

STORMGATE PRESS
QUICK READ BOOKS

MAKING READING FUN AGAIN!

STORMGATE PRESS
WWW.STORMGATEPRESS.COM

THE CONTRACT
Charles F. Millhouse

Shanghai, 1936

Sometimes in a man's life you reach a moment of pure clarity, where your whole life comes into focus, even more so with the barrel of a forty-four hanging inches from the end of your nose. After being shot, stabbed, and beaten up more times than I can count, the idea of death loses its intimidation.

"What will it be, Carrington?" Nickel asked in a nasally whistle.

Narrowing my eyes down the barrel of the revolver, I regarded the pale man. When he gave me an option, I realized he had no intention of pulling the trigger. Nickel Macintosh, or Nicky the Nose, was an Irish man who had most of his nose shot off in a card game several years ago. He wore a beat-up dark suit that he probably took off a dead man. He had filled his hair with too much Dapper Dan hair tonic, which he must have used to polish his leather shoes too.

Nickle was a two-bit thug who hired his gun out to anyone who had a score to settle. Don't take me wrong, while I might have painted a picture of him being a pushover, don't let him fool you. He's resourceful, well versed in torture, and he rather enjoys inflicting pain on other people. When he ambushed me in the alley at midnight behind Shin Wan Harry's, I should have realized he was working for someone who wanted me alive, at least for the time being.

I've pissed off a lot of people since I arrived in Shanghai, and there were enough people holding a grudge against me to make the list of those wanting to see me dead, rather long. In case you didn't know it, I'm a tramp steamer captain. My name's Zane Carrington, and my ship is the *Algiers*. I haul cargo all over Southeast Asia, sometimes legit, other times not so much.

Resting on my knees behind Harry's, I asked, "Are we going to stay out here all night, or are we going to get on with this?" The pressure from the pistol against my face intensified.

"Word on the street is you're sailing out of Shanghai on the morning tide," Nickle said.

"Where did you hear that?" I asked, trying not to corroborate his statement. "Besides what concern is it of yours?"

"It isn't any concern of mine," Nickle said snidely. "But it is a concern to my employer, who claims you have a standing contract with him."

Anger built inside me. Sometime last year, I entered into a contract with a man named Hugo Strangler. Agreeing to transport cargo for him with no questions asked. It seemed to be beneficial considering it was steady work, and he paid me well. It wasn't until I learned he wanted me to take part in human slavery that I refused. Swearing I would never work for him again.

If there was anyone in Southeast Asia that wanted to see me dead, it would be Strangler. He needed me for something, which is why I wasn't dead.

"He sent me to deliver a message to you," Nickle said.

I stared up into Nickle's eyes and said, "Are you going to give it to me, or are we going to stand around here all night?"

"Don't give me a reason to pull this trigger," Nickle said.

"Look Nose..."

"Don't call me that," Nickle barked, pulling back the hammer of his pistol.

"You going to give me the message or not?" I asked, irritated.

"Hugo said if you want out of your contract, you'll meet him tomorrow night and hear his proposition."

"What proposition?"

"If I knew, I sure as hell wouldn't tell you," Nickle said. "All I know is what I told you. You can either go or ignore the request, in which case the next time we meet it will be under different circumstances. It's your call, Carrington."

"As much as I've enjoyed our conversation tonight, Nickle, I'll meet Hugo..."

"You better," Nickle said, taking the gun away from my face. "Otherwise..."

"Yeah, yeah, yeah, I get the point," I said, standing. "Where does he want to meet?"

Nickle searched his memories, rolling his eyes back and forth in their sockets.

"Don't tell me you forgot?" I said.

"It will come to me," Nickle said.

"You, uh, want me to wait here while you go and ask him?" I said.

For a fleeting second, it looked like Nickle was going to take me up on that idea, until he shot me an irritated expression, and said, "Do you take me for a fool?"

"A dimwitted one at that," I said.

Nickle used the butt of his pistol to punch me in the gut, and when I bellied over, I found the barrel of it back in my face. "If I didn't have to keep you alive, Carrington, you would regret crossing me."

"Get in line, pal," I said, holding my stomach. "You going to remember where I'm meeting Hugo or not?"

"You know a place called the Black Dragon?" Nickle asked.

Nodding, I said, "Yeah, I know where it's at."

"Nine o'clock tomorrow evening, and don't be a minute late or I come looking for you."

I was in no position to argue, considering Hugo held that damn contract over my head. I know what you're thinking, and you would be right. A contract like the one Hugo had wasn't binding in a court, considering he wanted me to be a human trafficker. Only that's not how things work in Southeast Asia.

If I attempted to renege on the contract, Hugo would have no way to enforce it except by killing me. Only Hugo didn't work like that. He would prefer to tarnish my reputation by spreading the word that I backed out on a written agreement, which would cause me being branded as untrustworthy. And in my line of work, that meant a lot.

No one would trust me, and that meant no one would hire me again. Ever. Hugo would spread the word so far that even those whom I worked for in the past wouldn't take the chance of hiring me.

Assuring Nickle I would be at the Black Dragon the following evening, I bypassed Harry's. The last thing I wanted was a drink. Getting myself lost in a bottle wouldn't do me any good, and considering I've gone down that road before, it would only end in trouble, and I was in enough of that as it was.

The *Algiers* is my home. A tramp steamer built in 1924. She was a bit rusted, with splotches of dark green algae peeking above the waterline and an assortment of bullet holes littering her hulking metal frame. As you can tell by now, my life can be complicated, and if the battle scars on my boat weren't any sign, then Nicky the Nose pointing his pistol at my head should have done it.

With my ship at pier 18, and for a modest fee of a few copper coins that were worth less than their face value, I was able to call Shanghai my port of call. Some might think my current abode unappealing, but considering most every other port in the world could extradite me back to the States, I figured it would have to do. It's not paradise, but it's certainty better than a jail cell. If you don't know by now, I'm a wanted man for murder. Don't get me wrong, I'm not going to bore you with the details, but I'm guilty as charged.

If I hadn't gone off in a fit of revenge, I would be in New York now at my parent's estate. God, I miss that place. If I concentrated hard enough, I could hear my father on the phone trying desperately to keep a client out of jail. While my mother was baking something sweet in the kitchen and fussing with my brother and sister. It wasn't hard to imagine being there, but it was difficult keeping the illusion in my mind alive when my three crew members were hooting and hollering when I climbed up the gangplank to the deck of the ship.

Like most nights when we weren't hauling cargo, Lucas with no last name, and Crocker, my engineer, would drink, play music and have a good old time. For some apparent reason, Ronald P. Chesterton III, a retired major in the British army, joined them. It wasn't like Ronald to take part, but when the mood and the gin hit him, he could be as happy-go-lucky as any man. Don't let the neatly laundered and maintained suit from Ede and Ravenscroft of London fool you. Ronald had a dark side, and his stiff upper lip decorum was a front for secrets that I never pried in.

"Skipper," Lucas said with a bit of a slur in his tone. He tried to tuck in his gray tee-shirt in the cusp of his pants and run his fingers through his oily hair. He was always trying to impress me, even more so after he'd been drinking. "We figured you'd be out for the night."

Ronald stood from his chair and moved the needle off of the phonograph, leaving the sounds of the harbor to fill the air. "Zane," he said in a curious tone. "You look vexed."

"You get us a job, skipper?" Crocker asked. Undoubtedly, he consumed more alcohol than either the Major or Lucas combined but yet with a high constitution, Crocker seemed more sober than either of them. You couldn't figure that out by his appearance, considering Crocker always wore the same greasy coveralls, and only God Himself knew what he had on under them.

"No, no job," I replied.

"Then why back so early?" Lucas asked.

I thought about not telling them about my altercation with Nicky the Nose, but unlike most crews on most cargo ships, these three men were the closest thing I had to friends, and they would be upset if I at least didn't fill them in on the details.

"You've got to be kidding," Lucas said.

"I thought you were out from under Strangler when he went to prison," Crocker said.

"Men like that don't stay in prison," Ronald said. "Even men who sell their fellow man into slavery."

"Is this what this is all about?" Crocker asked. "Slavery?"

I reached for the almost empty bottle of gin on the table near Ronald and drunk down the rest of the swill. Allowing the burn to settle into my stomach, I said, "Nose mentioned the contract, so it might have something to do with that."

"That contract can't be binding," Ronald said.

The Major was right. But Southeast Asia had its own rules, and its own way of doing things. If any lawyer here in

Shanghai wanted to take on Strangler and attempt to break the contract, someone would pay them off to do a poor job, or worse, they would find themselves dead somewhere. Men like Hugo Strangler had a way of getting around the law, hence his short prison time. Whatever the reason Strangler wanted to see me, I'd be a fool not to go. I needed to face him, and if lucky, I'd put a bullet in him before he could screw me over.

After coming up with a somewhat rocky plan for meeting Hugo Strangler, I got some food in my stomach and some sleep, but after only four hours I heard Crocker hammering at my door and exclaiming, "Zane... Zane, we need you on deck... now."

I threw myself into the same clothes I was wearing only hours before and shoving my hair up under my peak cap I worked my way up to the deck to find uniformed police officers waiting for me. "What is this all about?" I demanded.

"Inspection," one officer said. He was clearly in charge and snapped his fingers, pointing ahead of him.

The men accompanying him fanned out into my ship and I stormed toward the man in charge and said, "We aren't hauling any cargo, so what's the meaning of this inspection?"

The lead officer's eyes went dark, and his jaw tightened, and he said with disdain in his tone, "We believe you are concealing contraband on this ship."

"Contraband... what sort of contraband?" I demanded.

The officer refused to answer, as he looked past me, waiting for his men. I turned toward Ronald, who offered me a grave look. He and I shared the same thought. Whatever they found on my ship, they were going to plant in here and I needed to be ready for anything.

"Tell me, officer, why did you pick out the *Algiers* to inspect? Was it something I said, or something I did, or both," I asked.

The officer didn't even look in my direction.

"I mean, I know I don't play by the rules sometimes," I said in a light tone. "But you can admit I keep things lively around here."

When I heard a high-pitched screech, I turned to find a shapely yet disheveled woman being led onto the deck. "Let me go," she screamed. She wasn't very old, probably nineteen or twenty, with ratty blond hair and deep blue eyes. She looked and sounded like an Australian. The green dress she wore was filthy and ripped at the shoulder. Whatever she had been through before she got onto my ship hadn't been kind to her.

"You are under arrest for human trafficking," the lead officer snapped, and before I knew it, Crocker, Lucas and Ronald were all being handcuffed.

"This is outrageous," I grumbled, but then realized I wasn't being cuffed like my friends and I said, "What's going on here?"

"Insurance," the officer told me.

It didn't take me a second to realize who was instigating this... Strangler, I thought. "Alright, what's he want?"

"Just to make sure you're going to be where you say you are," the officer said. "If you do not meet him, your three friends here will be convicted of slavery and thrown into a deep, dark hole."

My hands went into fists, and I eyed the situation carefully. When my gaze fell onto Ronald, he said, "Don't even think about it, boy."

By that time, it was too late. I didn't like being backed into a corner, and I didn't like my friends being treated as bait. Even though I couldn't do anything about them, I could make sure that Hugo Strangler would pay for his involvement with my friends.

I waited for my moment to act. For whatever reason, I didn't think what I was doing, but I knew the girl used in Strangler's game had to come with me. If anything, she could be nothing but a helpless pawn, or she could be complicit up to her eyeballs. Either way, she needed to come with me.

With little thought, I snagged the girl by the wrist and pulled her behind me as I rushed down the gangplank. She didn't struggle, and in fact she kept up with me pretty good. Having long legs, and a talent for moving pretty quickly, I didn't have trouble running. I'm glad that she didn't resist, because I'm not sure I could get away carrying her.

"Run, lad, run...!" Ronald shouted.

A police car was parked near the end of the ramp, and before I knew it, we both hopped into the car. Whoever this girl was, she didn't relish the idea of being left behind.

Bringing the engine alive, I slammed the car into first gear, released the clutch, and gave the engine gas as the automobile roared up the pier. The way ahead was clear, and with a quick check of the rearview mirror, behind us looked clear too. Which meant... they wanted me to escape. But I wasn't sure if I was supposed to take the girl with me or not and got me to thinking.

"Alright, spill it," I said, driving the car into the dawn of a new day.

"Spill what?" the girl asked.

"Strangler," I barked. "Are you working for him or..."

"For him?" the girl cut me down in a second. "He's filth."

By her tone she seemed sincere, but it was all confusing. Why put her on my ship? No doubt, to frame my friends so Strangler could secure my cooperation. He could have done that in several different ways.

Strangler knew me. I'm a bleeding heart for a pretty face, and this girl fit that criteria. Which made me believe she was a plant. But to what end? I wondered.

Turning the car down a backstreet, I parked it in the one place the cops wouldn't look for it. One block from the precinct. I know, I know it was a ballsy move and in fact I wasn't even sure if the police were looking for me, but I needed some answers, and I needed to ensure that we wouldn't be disturbed while I got them.

"Who are you?" I asked after turning off the car.

The girl regarded me. I wasn't sure if she was deciding if she could trust me or not. I mean, she got in the car with me, which meant she trusted me more than she did the cops. "I won't hurt you," I assured her.

"My name is Carol," she said, refraining from giving me a last name. "I was taken prisoner, along with several others, from the ocean liner Beauté de la mer."

"The Beauté de la mer sails in the South Pacific around French Polynesia," I said. "You're a long way from there."

"While in port, they abducted me with fifteen others. They drugged us and when I woke up, I found myself imprisoned in some room. I... I don't know where."

"And the others taken with you. Where are they?"

Carol rolled her shoulders, and she said, "I don't know."

By the tone of her voice, it sounded like she was telling the truth, but since coming to this part of the world, I've become jaded when it comes to people telling me the truth. If what she told me was true, then Hugo Strangler was up to his old schemes again. If that's the case, not only does he have me over a barrel, but he also has my friends as hostages. I looked at my watch. The sun was coming up, and it was going to make for a long hot day in a car.

Carol's face turned angry when I said, "If what you're telling me is the truth..." I backed down at her expression and added with an index finger in the air, "Look at it from my perspective. Several hours ago, I didn't know you from Eve, and now you're giving me a sob story. I don't know you; I don't really care to know you. But the man who did this to you has my friends. What if I told you there's a chance to get even with him? Are you willing to take that chance?"

Carol didn't ponder, not for a second, and replied with revenge in her tone, "What do you want me to do?"

For the next several hours, Carol and I worked out a plan. It was the kind of plan that you make up as you go along. Hugo Strangler was a narcissist and misogynistic and playing to those traits would be beneficial if I wanted to stay alive and get out from under this contract. Deep down I knew what he was going to ask and to tell you the truth, I would do it to save the lives of my friends. My agreement would, of course, be a part of my regular seat of the pants planning, and if I suspected Hugo of wanting another shipment of slaves, I would put an end it myself, and this time to *hell* with the law.

Evading the police was easy. I know enough people that wouldn't turn us in unless it was beneficial to them, so holding up until the evening was easy. I got a change of clothes for Carol. They weren't from some fancy store like Ede and Ravenscroft, but the plain gray dress was clean and fit her and that's all that mattered.

After a bath, and something to eat, I offered my friends money for their troubles, and soon Carol and I were on our way to the Black Dragon. It was a calculated risk taking her into the Dragon with me, but since I still didn't trust her, it was better to keep her where I could see her until I had a better idea of whose side she was on.

As soon as I walked into the Black Dragon, the clamor of Shanghai's night seemed to fall away. The restaurant was all shadows and whispers, a place where secrets were traded like currency. A rather hearty looking Asian man, who was missing his left eye met us at the door. He checked me for weapons and found none. I didn't stroll around Shanghai with a gun. Sure, I owned one but carrying it on my hip in the heart of Southeast Asia wasn't a smart thing to do, especially for a white man. That was just asking for trouble.

I spotted Hugo Strangler immediately, seated at a table in the far corner, his back to the wall, a position of power he never relinquished. He was dressed in a pristine white suit, the kind that made him stand out like a specter among the black-suited locals. His slick black hair was so well-groomed it looked like polished obsidian, and his dark eyes gleamed with a cunning that made my skin crawl.

Carol gripped my arm a little tighter as we approached him. I could feel the tension in her, a mirror of my own, but there was no turning back now. Hugo held the upper hand, and he knew it.

"Zane," he said smoothly, his voice like silk laced with venom. He gestured to the empty seats across from him. "Please, sit."

I sat down slowly, never taking my eyes off him. Carol slid in beside me, her hand still clutching my arm under the table. I could feel her trembling slightly, though she did her best to hide it.

"Hugo," I said, forcing my voice to stay steady. "What do you want?"

He smiled—a thin, sharp curve of his lips that didn't reach his eyes. "Straight to business. I like that about you, Zane. But you're forgetting the pleasantries. How's life treating you these days?"

"Cut the crap, Hugo. You didn't ask us here to exchange pleasantries."

His smile widened. "No, I suppose I didn't. But I do enjoy seeing you squirm a little. You always were too quick to push, Zane."

He leaned forward, steepling his fingers as he studied me. "The contract," he said, his voice dropping to a deadly whisper. "It's still in play, you know. One word from me, and you're finished. All of this..." he waved a hand vaguely in the air, "disappears. Gone."

I clenched my fists under the table. "What do you want?" I repeated.

Hugo's eyes flicked to Carol, who stiffened beside me. "I want you to remember your place. You and your charming companion here seem to think you can cross me and walk away unscathed. I'm here to remind you that isn't the case."

I could feel the fury rising in my chest, but I kept it in check. Hugo was dangerous, more dangerous than anyone I'd dealt with before. But he had one weakness: his arrogance.

"What's the play, Hugo?" I asked, my voice low and even. "You didn't drag us to the Black Dragon just to deliver a warning."

He leaned back, folding his arms across his chest. "No, I didn't," he admitted. "I have a job for you. Something... delicate. And you're going to do it, Zane, because if you don't, well, let's just say that contract will be the least of your worries."

I stared at him, my mind racing. There was no way out, not now. Hugo had me right where he wanted me, and he knew it.

"What's the job?" I asked, dreading the answer.

Hugo smiled again, a predatory gleam in his eyes. "Let us refrain from bullying one another. It will get us nowhere. Surely you know why you're here."

"I know why I'm here," I blurted out, reminding myself to be careful. "It's how you got me here that concerns me... especially after I told Nose I'd be here."

Strangler's eyebrows flared, and he said, "Nicky the Nose might be a trusting individual. I assure you I am not. After our past encounters, I felt I needed some insurance. I detained your friends as an assurance that you would show."

Not forgetting the guard behind me, I leaned forward in my seat, and Strangler put up his hand, telling his man to stand down. I glanced over my shoulder, and then directing my question to Strangler, I asked, "That's a pretty good trick, Hugo. Can you make him rollover and play dead, too?"

"Charming," Strangler replied. "I would be careful if I were you. Yen might not speak a lot of English, and he is very loyal to me, but there are no guarantees I can keep him under control."

With that knowledge, I kept my insults to a minimum. We were getting nowhere and even though I was becoming impatient, I had my friends to consider. "So, where do I pick up my cargo?" I asked.

"Your cargo? I don't understand," Hugo said.

"That's why I'm here. You're back in the slave trade, and you need me to—"

"Please, please, Zane. You're jumping to conclusions," Hugo said with a glib smile. "I assure you, after the last time I tried to get you to make a delivery of goods, it didn't work out so well."

"Is that how you see people, as goods?" I asked.

"I see them as money. And you caused me to lose a lot," Hugo said. "But that is water under the bridge."

"Then what do you want?" I asked.

Hugo poured himself a glass of wine and placed the stem of the glass between his index and middle fingers of his left hand. "In two months, I am to host a very particular card game that will fetch me a considerable amount of money," he said. "But the prize for that game is out of my reach. Or was out of my reach until I secured her." he gestured his hand toward Carol.

Glancing between them, I stopped and studied Carol, and asked, "What's so important about you?"

Judging by the look on Carol's face, there was more she wasn't telling me. By the glare in her eyes, she was keeping something to herself, and when Hugo said, "Allow me to introduce you to Ms. Carol Malcolm. The daughter of General Douglas Malcolm of the First Fighting Regiment. The General is unaware of his daughter's disappearance because he is stationed abroad, and the news has not reached him. Which is good news for you, Zane."

"Is this true?" I asked, turning toward Carol.

Looking past me, Carol fixed her eyes on Strangler, and said in a hard voice, "He has my brother, too."

Staring at her in disbelief, I put my mind to work, and when I turned back to Strangler, I said, "I demand to know what this is all about."

"General Malcolm is on an expedition as we speak," Strangler said. "Mapping the interior of the Mexican jungle. He's very fond of maps, your father, isn't he, my dear?"

"You sicken me," Carol said.

Ignoring her, Strangler continued by saying, "Right now, General Malcolm is mounting an expedition into the Yucatán Peninsula and set sail two days ago."

"I could be wrong," I said. "But wouldn't the Mexican government have a problem with the Australian army skulking around in their jungle?"

"Who said it was sanctioned?" Strangler replied. "My sources tell me he's looking for the remains of a lost Mayan tribe in the Amazon."

"The Amazon... there're no Mayans in the Amazon, Hugo."

"That's why it's called lost," Strangler said. "Seems they abandoned their people to worship the way they chose, some powerful goddess or something."

I eyed Hugo, having known him long enough. He wouldn't be interested in General Malcolm unless there was something in it for him. "What aren't you telling me?" I asked.

Strangler's lips curled up into a cunning smile. "General Malcolm is searching for a map, and he believes it's in Chichén Itzá."

"What's that?"

"Chichén Itzá was a mecca for the Mayan civilization that existed around eight to nine hundred AD," Strangler said. His eyes sparkled in voracity. "It was rediscovered in 1841, and its great pyramid, El Castillo, hasn't been completely explored. It's believed that the ancient map of Eloy, a High Priest who was the only man who knew the location of the lost tribe, exists in the pyramid. I want that map… I need that map, and if you want out of our contract, you need to go to Chichén Itzá and find it."

"Are you out of your mind?" I asked bitterly. "You expect me to travel halfway around the world, looking for a map that may or may not exist in a virtually unexplored pyramid, find it and deliver it to you in two months' time?"

"Yes," Strangler said. "You're the perfect man for this job."

That wasn't entirely true, the one man more suited for this job was Steven Hawklin, but if I was a betting man, which I can be from time to time, I wouldn't be surprised if Captain Hawklin already fits into this outlandish plan in some way.

"You expect me to do this without a crew?" I asked. "I need them to help run the *Algiers*, otherwise my ship isn't going anywhere."

Strangler thought about that for a moment, and said, "Alright, I will release your crew."

"And my brother?" Carol asked, but there wasn't a sense of urgency in her tone.

"Now you know I cannot do that, my dear. I expect you to accompany Zane on this journey. Besides, what better way to distract General Malcolm than with his own daughter?"

Carol huffed, and by her body language, she didn't like the idea at all, and I wasn't too fond of it myself.

"And what about me?" I asked.

"You never gave me an answer," Strangler said. "You'll do it? You'll go find this map?"

"Only if you promise to destroy my contract at the end of this," I said.

Strangler didn't take time to consider his answer, and without reservation said, "Yes, I will have it with me when you deliver the map in two months at the Hotel Cartagena."

"Cartagena," I muttered. "This just keeps getting better and better. That doesn't give me a lot of time, you know."

Strangler didn't offer a response, and after a long moment of silence, and with little choice, I said, "We have a deal."

Strangler reached out a hand. Staring at it, I said, "Don't push it, rat."

Strangler offered a thin grin and said, "Once you return to your ship, your crew will be waiting."

I thought about offering an idle threat, like they better be, or I'm warning you. But instead, I got the hell out of there before I did something stupid. I do that from time to time.

"I'll send along with your crew all the information I have obtained in this matter," Strangler said, and he added, "I look forward to working with you, Zane."

When I left the restaurant, I felt like I needed a shower.

ZANE CARRINGTON

Carol and I arrived back at the pier near the *Algiers* half an hour after leaving the Black Dragon. I didn't say much to her since then, mostly because I wasn't sure I trusted her. I kept getting this feeling as if she wasn't telling me everything, and I learned a long time ago, people kept secrets. In this part of the world, even more so.

"Zane, Zane," Lucas shouted from the deck of my ship.

I offered a wave of my own but stopped walking. "Prepare to get underway," I yelled. "I'll be on board in a minute."

"You mean we will be on board," Carol said.

"You're not going," I said bluntly.

"Why the hell not?" Carol asked in an abrasive tone.

I didn't mince words, and not sparing her feelings, I said, "Because I don't know what your part in all of this is."

"He has..."

"Your brother, yeah, so you said. But I'm not sure that's the truth. Hell, as far as I know, this General Malcolm isn't your father and you're working for Hugo."

Carol drew back a hand to slap me, but I caught it in mid-swing. "Tell me why I should trust you," I said.

"You're hurting me..." Carol said in a painful voice.

"I'll break your damned wrist if you don't answer my question," I said.

Dumbfounded, Carol regarded me for a few seconds before she said, "You're right. You're right. You shouldn't trust me. But he has my brother, and if I don't go along with you on this quest to find my father, he will kill William. Do you have any idea what that means?"

Keeping hold of her wrist for a long few seconds, I finally let go of her. She withdrew, rubbing her wrist in her other hand.

It's not that I didn't want to trust her, because I wanted to, especially if she was indeed the daughter of General Malcolm, only she could identify him. But there were too many variables in play that could sink not only me, but my ship. If what she told me was true, and I didn't allow her to come, and her brother died... well, that was something I was pretty sure I could live with.

"I'm taking a big gamble here," I said. "If for one moment you lead me to believe you are not on the up and up, I will chuck you over the side of my ship so fast you won't have time to scream before you hit the ocean."

"I swear to you everything I have told you is the truth and if I don't go along, Strangler will undoubtedly kill my brother," Carol said as water welled in the bottom of her eyes.

Most men would be a sucker when a woman cried in front of them. I was not that type of man. Oh, sure, sometimes I melted at the sign of a woman crying, but this wasn't one of those times. Call it a sixth sense or call it what you will, but something down deep inside me told me not to trust this woman, and when I said, "Alright, you can come along," I was already regretting it.

The *Algiers* set sail thirty minutes later, and once we were out of the harbor, I brought the engines to full steam and set our course for the Yucatan Peninsula. We were twenty days away from the Panama Canal, and then another two days before we could drop anchor. With ample provisions, we hunkered in for the long voyage ahead.

"I've only heard of General Malcolm," Ronald told me when he and I had time to talk.

"Does he have any children?" I asked, hoping to find out if what I'd been told was true.

Ronald stuffed his pipe with a sweet-smelling tobacco, and before striking a match said, "I couldn't tell you, lad."

"I didn't think so."

"Now, if I had met the man, maybe I could answer that. But most men in the service don't talk much about family, kids and the like. Most military men, especially career members, keep their personal lives to themselves."

It was funny, but Ronald never spoke of his family. I never thought too much about a wife, or children, but after his statement of soldiers keeping their private lives to themselves, I wondered.

The Major and I began studying the information Strangler provided. There were no pictures of the General, or anyone accompanying him on his expedition, but there was a map provided.

General Malcolm would put ashore near Río Lagartos, Mexico. A small coastal town with little inhabitants, but a place to supply before going into the interior. I planned to make landfall near El Cuyo, a fishing community. The fewer people that found us coming ashore, the better, the last thing I wanted to do was raise suspicion with the local police. There, we would get fresh water and supplies before making our journey across the thick jungle. The entire peninsula was vastly unexplored and while I believe we would come across several small villages on our journey, the entire area would be virtually uninhabited.

Over the prevailing weeks, I saw little of Carol Malcolm. She took most of her meals away from the rest of us and stayed on deck, either reading or staring out at the open sea. I refrained from striking up a conversation with her mostly because I didn't want to become invested in her, nor did I want my feelings swayed. I'd learned over several years to distance myself from anyone that could influence my decisions in life, and it helped keep my mind clear of influence. Think of me as heartless if you wish, but there was no room in my life for someone I did not trust, and besides my crew, I trusted no one.

Young Lucas kept me company in the wheelhouse on most days. He was quickly becoming a proficient navigator and took to his life on the sea far better than I did when I first joined the crew of the *Algiers*. We shared stories of life in America, even though his stories were missing minor details, and I didn't pry. He had his reasons for distancing himself from his life before I found him hiding on my ship.

I had been on the open sea before, but never in this part of the world. The endless ocean stretched out before me, an expanse of shimmering blue that seemed to merge with the sky at the horizon. Standing on the deck of the *Algiers*, I felt the familiar creak of the old steamer beneath my boots. Its rusted metal sides worn by years of battling the elements. The salty breeze carried the scent of freedom and adventure, and as I looked out over the waves, I could see the sun's reflection dancing on the water like a thousand diamonds scattered across the surface.

The vastness of the sea never failed to remind me of how small we truly are in the grand scheme of things. Out here, far from the bustling ports and crowded cities, the world felt wild and untamed. The ocean was a living, breathing thing—its moods shifting from calm serenity to fierce storms in the blink of an eye. As the *Algiers* cut through the waves, and the sea slammed the side of my vessel, it was a constant reminder that we were but visitors in this enormous, mysterious domain—the open ocean was both a challenge and a refuge and out here I felt more alive than anywhere else on Earth.

We arrived off the coast of Mexico on the night of September 8th. There was a stale breeze on the air, hot and foreboding that weighed heavily down on us. By daybreak we armed ourselves with revolvers, machetes and rifles. We left Crocker on the *Algiers*, as the rest of us rowed ashore in a small boat. The sun fully rose over the horizon as we reached shore. We quickly unloaded our supplies. To my surprise, the Major took point, stating, "I've been on plenty of expeditions like this. Follow my lead."

I received a curious glance from Lucas, who seemed as astonished as me. For the last couple of years, Ronald Chesterton barely went ashore in Shanghai, let alone get wrapped up in any of my hair-brained schemes. I wasn't sure if he understood the severity of what was happening, or that he knew how important it was to me to get out from under Hugo Strangler. Whatever the case, I was proud of the old man. In all reality, I assumed he missed the army life, and his beloved England and this was a way of reliving all those campaigns he told me about.

Not long after we left the beach and went inland, we spotted movement ahead of us.

"I thought you said this part of Mexico was mostly uninhabited," Carol said in a whisper.

Suspicious, I ignored her and told everyone to wait as I moved forward. We were near the fishing village of El Cuyo, but upon further scrutiny, I found myself staring at non-Hispanics. They dressed in khakis, and although they didn't wear any insignia, I suspected they were neither Australians nor Americans. The hairs stood up on the back of my neck, and I couldn't shake the feeling they were not here for the tourist season. Luckily, they were turning away from the village, and I breathed a little easier, since we needed to stop there just long enough to pick up some supplies.

Returning to the others, I relayed what I saw, and when the Major said, "Something's wrong... what is it?"

Taking a moment to collect my thoughts, I said, "Hugo wasn't very forthcoming about who else was involved with this search. But by their dress and mannerisms, I can't rule out that..."

"That what?" Ronald asked.

I didn't want to say it out loud, and by not doing so eased my anxiety. Something as important as this map to some lost Mayan city was too important to be ignored by other powers in the world... especially if it held secrets, secrets that could benefit those countries arming for war. "Maybe you should go back to the ship Major, Lucas and I..."

"Nonsense," Ronald replied. "I didn't get dressed in my best expedition outfit and don my favorite pith helmet to turn around and go back to the ship. We press on."

Carol came in close to me, and in a guarded tone she asked, "You think they're Germans, don't you?"

Taken aback, I asked, "What makes you say that?" I stared into Carol's eyes searching for answers."

"It makes sense is all," Carol said. "There must be other interested parties if this map does lead to a lost Mayan city."

I didn't offer a reply, and instead I regarded Carol waiting for her to reveal something.

"If they were Germans, do you think they know about my father?"

"Most probably," I said. "But one thing's for sure, I doubt they know about us–" I paused and asked, "What about you... do you want to go back to the ship?"

For a moment I thought she was going to say yes, but with only seconds to think about it, she proved me wrong by saying, "No, I go with you. My father has to know what is going on." She rolled her eyes away from me, looking to the ground at our feet. It was at that moment that she revealed herself. She knew more than she was telling me, and I couldn't fight the feeling that we were walking into a trap.

After gaining food, water and some other needed supplies, we began our journey by midday. As we pressed on, it didn't take long to realize that the Mexican jungle ahead of us, wasn't like any other jungle I'd been in before. Dense and unwelcoming, it seemed endless, an oppressive sea of green swallowing us whole as we hacked our way through the thick underbrush. The air was heavy with humidity, each breath feeling like I was inhaling steam. The Major continued to lead as Lucas and Carol followed closely behind, their faces a mixture of determination and weariness. We remained alert, scanning the foliage for any sign of movement. Somewhere out there amongst the green was Carol's father, and a third party that I hoped wasn't Germans, or any other hostile party.

Over the next several days, we covered nearly twenty miles with a mixture of flat grassland and rocky hills that slowed our progress. Carol said little during that time, keeping to herself. I didn't pry, but I sure as hell wanted to. Whatever she was keeping from us was going to fall on us like a ton of bricks and I didn't like that idea, not one damn bit.

On the sixth day of our travel, we spotted smoke in the distance. "Campfire do you think?"

Ronald shook his head. "Probably a village," he said. "I'd say they're fifteen, maybe twenty miles away."

"Locals are the least of our worries," I said.

"Don't be too sure. How would you feel if you found white men traipsing around in your backyard?" Ronald asked.

"Hostile, do you think?"

"Perhaps. We should be cautious."

"Hostile locals are the least of our worries," Lucas said.

Looking into Lucas' glassy eyes, I asked, "What's that mean?"

"Carol's gone."

My hand went to the hilt of my pistol, and I scoured the surrounding area. "What do you mean, gone?"

"As in not here," Lucas said.

"Alright, let's fan out and see if we can find her," Ronald said. "She may have just wondered off. She's probably not too far away."

I didn't share the Major's optimism, but I gave Carol the benefit of the doubt. The three of us went in different directions, understanding that we would meet back in ten minutes.

I didn't go far as I passed through the overgrowth and I saw the back of Carol's head through the foliage. She was standing incredibly still, and I changed my course to approach her from the side. My heart pounded in my chest when I came out of the thicket, my eyes locked on Carol, who stood frozen in terror a few yards away. Between us, a rather large wild boar stood, his ferocious snorting raised the hair on my arms.

I could feel the sweat trickle down my back, the weight of my decision pressing heavily on my shoulders. There was no turning back now. Carol needed me, and despite how I felt about her, or what secrets she was keeping from me, I swore to myself that she would come to no harm. I tightened my grip on the worn handle of the rifle, praying it wouldn't jam at this crucial moment.

"Carol," I whispered, barely audible over the distant calls of the wildlife. "Stay still. Don't move." Her eyes, wide with fear, flicked to mine. She nodded imperceptibly, her breath coming in quick, shallow gasps.

The boar's muscles tightened as it buried its front hoof into the sod. It was preparing to charge. I removed the rifle from my back and raised it ever so gently, my hands shaking slightly as I took aim. The boar paused; its ears twitching as it sensed the change in the air. For a moment, our eyes met, and I could see the raw power and primal instinct in its obsidian depths. This magnificent creature was simply following its nature, but so was I.

"Easy now," I murmured to myself, steadying my aim. I took a deep breath, focusing all my concentration on the swine. One shot, I told myself. One shot to save her. The crack of the rifle echoed across the prairie, startling a flock of birds into the sky. The pig squealed in pain and surprise, leaping into the air before collapsing onto its side. I stood there, breathless, my heart pounding in my ears as the dust settled. For a moment, there was only silence. Then, slowly, Carol moved, her steps tentative at first. I rushed to her side, my legs feeling like jelly beneath me. She threw her arms around me, her body trembling against mine. "Zane," she whispered, her voice choked with emotion. I held her tight, feeling the adrenaline ebb away, leaving me weak and shaky.

With barely enough time to slow my heartbeat, Ronald and Lucas appeared through the dense jungle, their looks defeated and unnerving. When a rather large man with thick black muttonchops appeared from behind them, he pushed himself past, exclaiming, "Carol! What the devil are you doing here?"

ZANE CARRINGTON

We arrived at the campsite of the Australian expedition, after dark. Lucas, Carol, and I were placed under guard in a makeshift tent and provided with food and water. Carol refused to eat. To say that she was cold towards her father would have been an understatement. I had seen snowmen with warmer hearts.

"Why did they take the Major?" Lucas asked.

"Military men recognize military men, I suppose," I said. It was probably for the better, considering I have a tendency to offer off-color remarks that might get us in deeper trouble. Ronald had a panache for saying the right things, and I knew he would smooth things over with the General. He seemed the man that would understand the situations and...

With General Malcolm hot on his heels, Ronald was forcefully shoved into the tent. The Major appeared physically fit, but by his expression, emotionally stressed. Carol stepped toward the back of the tent trying to hide herself from her father, masking herself in the lantern's dim light.

The General set his eyes on her for a few seconds, before turning his gaze on me. With his eyes hooded, he said, "Seems you're here to rob me of my triumph."

"Rob is harsh, General," I said. "I look at it as a means to an end."

"How so?" Malcolm asked.

"I need the map you seek for two reasons..."

"Zane, maybe you should listen to the General, first," Ronald spoke up.

I wish I hadn't ignored him, but I needed to make the General see reason. Sure, the map would get me out from under Strangler, which I desperately wanted, and I would make sure I explained that to him in due course, but no man would allow his son to remain captive, especially by a man like Hugo Strangler.

"My son has been dead for two years," Malcolm said in a harsh, unforgiving tone. "So, I don't give a damn what trouble you might have gotten yourself into with this Strangler character."

I turned toward Carol. Her expression had turned malevolent. With wicked eyes, she took a step toward me. I don't know why, but in that split second, I realized I was staring at the personification of evil, and General Malcolm said, "She murdered my son William. His own sister." My stomach sank, and I was suddenly transported back to that horrific time when I discovered my beloved Diana's body on the steps of her parent's home. It's an emotion I cannot even try to explain. My whole body turned icy cold, and it took everything I had not to reach out for Carol Malcolm and strangle the life out of her. "You're working for Hugo Strangler."

"I had you all fooled," Carol said with a sinister smile. "Hugo needed insurance. He wasn't sure you could get the job done Zane, and I came along to make sure you did."

"I should have allowed that boar to have its meal," I said harshly. "Even if you would have left a sour taste in his mouth."

"General," Ronald's voice was overshadowed by my seething heartbeat, and as I fought the internal rage, he said,

"We were not aware this woman caused you so much grief. We were under the assumption..."

Malcolm raised a hand and said, "I don't know how she escaped from the sanitarium, but I assure you she will be going back there. As for the map–"

Correcting my footing, I turned toward Malcolm and said, "Never mind, General. That map's no longer important to me. I'm going to kill Hugo Strangler. That's the only way I'll ever be out from under him."

"Zane, do you know what you're saying?" Lucas asked.

"Hugo Strangler is more than just a criminal," I barked. "He's a monster, a man who profits off the suffering of others and for reasons I can barely admit to myself, I signed a contract with him. A contract that has bound me to his hideous operations in human trafficking."

"I can't live with that," I said, my voice rising with determination. "I won't live with that. I've tried to find a way out to sever ties without causing more harm, but Strangler hasn't made it easy. There's only one way this ends: either I remain his pawn, or I take his life."

Before anyone could react to my affirmation, gunshots rang outside the tent. Shouts in German resonated throughout the encampment. "Lucas," I shouted, pointing at one of the lanterns, as I doused the light in the oil lamp nearest me.

I turned on Carol, keeping my anger in check, and said, "You knew they were Germans, didn't you?"

"Hugo knew the Germans were interested in the map," Carol said. "Hell, even one player in Hugo's card game is a German general. Hugo thought they would try coming after the map and avoiding the card game. Seems he was right."

"They have been shadowing us for days," Malcolm said, kneeling down near the entrance of the tent. "I had my suspicions it was Germans ghosting us, but until now, I wasn't sure."

"Why attack now?" I asked.

"We discovered the Mayan Pyramid this morning. I guess they don't want to share the discoveries with us."

"Not that you're going to share," I said.

"What do you think?" General Malcolm asked.

"Despite what you might think, General, you and I are not enemies," I assured him.

Malcolm's piercing eyes glared at me in the dark, and he was trying to figure out what kind of man I was to bring his lunatic daughter to him in such an inhospitable place. I couldn't blame him; I was trying to figure this all out for myself.

"We have a common enemy," I said. "Let me help you fight them."

"Your weapons are two tents over," Malcolm said. "We might not make it."

"We don't appear to have a lot of choices," I said.

Malcolm pivoted his body, regarded Lucas, Ronald and me and said, "Follow me and keep low." He bolted from the tent, and I went out after him.

Weapon flashes sparked the dying night and cries of death followed. Turning, I waved Lucas and Ronald ahead, and they followed the General closely as I reached a hand out for Carol. She might be deranged and confused, but she didn't deserve to be left to the cruelty of the German invaders.

Carol paused, wide eyed—her features twisted and choleric. "What are you doing?" I asked.

Frantic, Carol's eyes darted around the encampment, flickering from shadow to shadow as if the darkness itself whispered secrets only she could hear. Her hands trembled, clutching at the worn fabric of her skirt with a white knuckled grip. The surrounding air seemed to charge, buzzing with a palpable tension that set my nerves on edge.

"Carol," I called softly, stepping closer, my voice a gentle plea. "Come with me, let me help you... This place is not safe."

Her gaze snapped to mine and for a moment I saw a flicker of recognition, a glimmer of the woman that seemed sane when I first met her. But it was gone as quickly as it appeared.

"You don't understand," she hissed, her voice barely more than a whisper but filled with a desperate intensity. "You're like him, you're like my father. Wanting to take me back, wanting to put me away... put me away and forgetting about me."

I reached out, trying to bridge the gap between us. "You can't stay here, Carol. Do you know what the Germans will do to you if they find you?"

She turned and walked away from me—her movements were jerky and uncoordinated, like a puppet with cut strings. I took several steps after her; the Germans were everywhere. Why they hadn't found us yet was beyond me, and it was only a matter of seconds until they did. "Carol." I pleaded, "Let me help you."

She stopped, her back to me, her shoulders shaking with silent sobs. I reached out again, this time more cautiously, but before I could touch her, she spun around, eyes wide with fear and fury.

"I can't stay here!" she cried, the sound raw and primal. "I have to go now. Before he puts me back there, I have no other choice!"

Carol, no–"

But she was already gone, bolting into the night with a speed born of pure panic. I could only watch as she disappeared into the night, her terrified screams echoing in my ears long after she was out of sight.

Weapon's fire rung out in her direction. Had the Germans discovered her? I wondered. I stood there for a handful of heartbeats, knowing I could not pursue her. When the shadows of an armed man came into view, I knew I had to run.

Sprinting after the others, I came face to face with General Malcolm, who glared over my shoulder, not surprised that his daughter was not behind me. "I couldn't stop her," I said.

Without a word, Malcolm thrust my Smith and Wesson gun belt into my hands and, not missing a beat, said, "Follow me."

We rushed into the new day dawn as muzzle flashes lit up the dying night behind us, and it wouldn't take the Germans long to realize that General Malcolm had fled.

The only advantage we had was, the Nazis knew nothing about me, or my people.

Beside me, General Malcolm led our small group with determination. Lucas and Ronald followed closely behind, their faces a mixture of that same determination combined with a growing weariness. I worried about the Major. He was a seasoned war veteran, but his age slowed him down and with gunshots back in the camp growing silent, slowing down wasn't an option.

We remained vigilant, scanning the foliage for any sign of movement. It wouldn't take long for the Germans to catch up to us.

This rumor of an ancient map that would lead to a lost city of Mayans in the heart of the Amazon had seemed absurd at first, but with General Malcolm and the Germans here searching for it, they added some credence to the legend.

It was a race against time with unprecedented stakes. Not only was my own safety on the line, but I also had to stay ahead of the villains to protect my crew.

"Keep your eyes peeled," Malcolm muttered, his voice low but authoritative. "If the Germans find that map before us, there's no telling what they'll do. Regardless, I have prepared for such a contingency."

"What does that mean?" I asked.

"I'm a military man, and as such, I'm am prepared for anything," Malcolm said. "I had my men plant explosives all over this area. If I can't have the map, then no one can."

Speechless, I watched the General push his way ahead. I couldn't blame him. He was on a mission, and so were the

Germans. I had encountered Germans before, the really nasty ones, and I knew their cruelty.

The idea of the Germans getting the upper hand on any kind of weapon, ancient or otherwise, sent my mind into a frenzy, but I cleared my thoughts of that notion, since I was going to use the map to get me out of the predicament that I was in with Hugo Strangler, and damn the consequences.

Ronald, ever the optimist, tried to lighten the mood with his confidence. "We'll get there first. We have to." Just as he spoke, Lucas raised his hand, signaling us to stop.

"Do you hear that?" he asked, his voice barely above a whisper. We all strained our ears, and then I heard it—a faint chanting, carried on the wind.

It was a sound unlike anything I'd ever heard—rhythmic and almost hypnotic, sending a chill down my spine. We advanced carefully toward its source, our senses sharp. When we finally emerged from the dense undergrowth, we were awestruck. As we neared the jungle's edge, Chichén Itzá appeared before us, breathtakingly majestic. The Pyramid of El Castillo stood like a stone sentinel amidst the verdant expanse, its steps ascending toward the sky in a way that felt almost surreal.

The morning sunbathed the ancient structure in a golden light, making the shadows dance across its surface as if the spirits of the past were still alive, still guarding their secrets. I glanced over at Ronald, his usual composure replaced by a look of awe. For a man who'd seen the wonders of Egypt and the splendor of Rome, this was something new—something different. Lucas had gone silent by the sheer grandeur before us. There was reverence in his eyes, a quiet respect that spoke volumes. For me, I couldn't help but wonder what secrets it held, what stories were etched into its stones, waiting to be uncovered. We stood there for what felt like hours, letting the sight sink in, each of us lost in our own thoughts. I felt a mixture of excitement and trepidation. This place had brought us here for a purpose, and I couldn't shake the sense that it held more than we could possibly foresee. Rediscovered less than a century ago, we were fortunate that no local archaeological teams were currently stationed nearby.

"Where did that chanting come from?" General Malcolm asked as we neared the cusp of the pyramid.

"Ghosts," I said in a serious tone, catching a skeptical eye from the General.

"This is incredible," Lucas whispered, his eyes wide with wonder. "How could this have been lost for so long?"

"History has its secrets," Ronald replied, his voice tinged with awe.

As we crossed the length of the pyramid, we worked our way deeper into the ancient ruins when Lucas said, "There it goes again. Do you hear that?"

The chants were low, but as we moved forward, they progressively grew louder.

We followed the eerie hymns, our steps quickening, driven by a mixture of fear and determination. The closer we got, the more I felt a strange energy in the air, a sense of something ancient and powerful. The chanting drew us to a smaller stone structure, reaching a massive entrance, its doorway guarded by the imposing statue of what I later learned was Kukulcan, the serpent god.

The chanting was coming from within. Ronald motioned for us to stay back as he crept forward, peering inside. He turned back to us, his face pale. "They aren't ghosts at all, but more Germans," he said, his voice barely audible. "They're performing some kind of ritual."

"What kind of ritual?" Malcolm asked.

"Damned if I know," Ronald replied. "But it's not good."

"How many did you see?" I asked.

"About a dozen," Ronald replied.

"Not counting those back in your camp, General. We are sorely outnumbered," Lucas said.

"That's nothing new for us," I replied.

Taking a deep breath, we charged into the structure, weapons at the ready, surprising the Germans as we entered. The scene erupted into chaos—shouts from the bewildered German mystics as their eerie chanting ceased. Unarmed, they faced us without fear. At the center of the structure stood an ancient altar, its surface adorned with intricate carvings that seemed to emit a strange, otherworldly glow. On the altar lay the map we were searching for, its details faintly illuminated in the dim light. "Looks like the German expedition has been here longer than you thought, General," I remarked.

Malcolm, stunned, replied, "That's impossible."

"They've been here long enough to find the map and beat you to it, General," Ronald said.

The German leader stepped forward, a striking figure with sharp, elongated features. He wore elaborate robes in black and white, prominently displaying a swastika at the center of his chest. His commanding presence and the meticulous detail of his attire underscored his authority and the gravity of the situation.

"How is that possible?" The General asked. "My team and I have been here nearly a week. We saw nothing of them until tonight. They couldn't have been here all this time. How did they find the map so quickly?"

"You fools!" the Nazi high priest spat in English. "Our being here is not by accident, but providence. We are ordained by God. We sought the map for the greater good. It called to us. You don't know what you're meddling with!"

"It doesn't take a genius to figure it out," I shot back, raising my pistol.

"The map will lead us to treasures beyond imagination," the ceremonial figure said. "But for you, for you, it will only bring death!" He produced a pistol from the folds of his robes.

None of us hesitated, but when we pulled the triggers of our weapons... nothing happened. Lucas chomped down on a curse word, and when the Major and I shared a quizzical look, the ground rumbled and quaked. A fantastic shudder knocked us to the ground.

"What the hell is happening?" General Malcolm exclaimed.

Each time I tried to stand, the earth dropped out from under me, and I plummeted back to the floor in a staggering wallop, and it didn't take me long to realize the worst was yet to come.

Great fissures ripped across the temple floor, and before any of us could figure out was happening, the skeletal frames of the dead climbed out of the earth. The shredded remains of Mayan ceremonial clothing adorned the apparitions standing before us, armed with impressive cudgels cut from the remains of a mahogany tree and stained red from blood. Alive, these people were once tall and formidable, but dead, their supernatural presence was frightening and ominous. It didn't take a genius to realize that these were once high priests of the temple, out to protect their sacred map at any cost.

"You will be but the first to fall at the might of our newfound power!" the German priest exclaimed. "Once we leave this place, and find the lost city of the Mayans, will the world face the true might of German superiority!"

When the quakes subsided, I snagged the Major by the arm and lifted him from the floor. There was a moment of calm before the German priest shouted, "They have defiled this sacred place... Kill them!" He then spoke in a dialect unfamiliar to me, sending the skeletal apparitions into a frenzy.

Charging us, the skeletons came forward, lashing their clubs as they approached. General Malcolm took a blow to the head instantly that knocked him off his feet. Pulling Ronald with me, I kept out of striking range, but the animated bones raced toward us, nimble – their hollow eye sockets void of life.

Lucas used his rifle as a club, swinging it right, left, and right again. He kept out of arm's length, but yelled, "I can't keep this up for long...!"

Without hesitation, I moved forward and tackled two of the reanimated figures, just like I used to back in my college football days. We slammed to the ground and one of the

Skeltons shattered bones scattered the floor, and I got to my feet before the surviving apparition came at me. To my surprise, those bones that had shattered to the floor reformed, pulling itself back together, rebuilding itself one bone at a time until the skeletal warrior stood before me once again.

"Zane!" Ronald yelled. "The priest!"

The German high priest stood in a trance, surrounded by his sycophants. He held his hands out over them as they returned to their eerie chanting. Their words were in German, and I didn't have to speak it to understand they were offering their essence, their very lives to him and it was clear he was controlling his skeletal army.

Rushing forward, I barreled my way through the line of Mayan phantasms, smashing them as I went. I only had one chance before the skeletons reformed, and I dove through the air over the priest's minions, grabbing him by the crook of his neck, shoving him to the floor under me. Grabbing the eight-inch knife blade at my side, I plunged it deep into the priest's chest; his eyes filled with surprise, he stared at me in disbelief.

I don't know how to explain what happened next, but without the lack of a better term, an effervescent glow exploded from the German's chest. It engulfed the temple, washing through the structure like an ocean wave.

Burying my head in my arms, blocking my eyes from the blinding light, I remained there until I heard Ronald call to everyone, "It's alright, lads. It's over."

Barely having time to get to my feet, weapons fire barked outside the temple. I turned toward General

Malcolm, but he was gone. "Lucas, grab your gun," I said, finding my pistol only inches from me. "The General has this whole area rigged with explosives. We have to find him before he sets them off."

Ronald followed, but stopping him, I said, "Get the map. Lucas and I will see what's going on outside." Without hesitation, Ronald nodded and turned toward the altar.

Outside, was quiet. Even the sounds of the jungle had grown silent. "What do we do, Zane?" Lucas asked.

"We get the hell out of here," I replied. My thoughts went to the Germans who attacked Malcolm's camp, and figured they had to be close by.

Ronald appeared a few seconds later with a silver tube in his hands. "I have the map," he said, shaking the tube in his fist, and before I could say, let's get back to the *Algiers*, the temple erupted in a series of triggered explosions.

"It's the General!" I shouted as Lucas, Ronald, and I ran away from the collapsing temple. Stone, mortar and ash tumbled to the ground as a continuous bombardment of explosions littered the temple sight—great chunks of dirt, filled the air with dense debris, making it difficult to see.

"Where are we going?" Ronald shouted.

"Keep running!" I yelled.

"What?" Lucas screamed.

"I said, keep running!"

The ground trembled, and the remnants of the eruptions marred the cottony red glow of a new day, filtering out the sun. We scurried down an embankment outside the pyramid of sight and paused just long enough to catch our breath.

"Where's... where's the General?" Lucas asked between breaths.

"Caught in the explosions, I would assume," Ronald said as he rested on his back.

"If only it was that simple," I added, staring into the end of General Malcolm's pistol.

Lucas and Ronald scrambled to their knees, but the General quickly warned, "I will not hesitate to shoot him."

"You're going to shoot me anyway," I said, trying not to show my fear. "I saw it in your eyes when we first met."

"I'm not the murderous type," Malcolm replied. "I am the type that doesn't like to lose, so if killing you is how I accomplish that, so be it."

"Why, General?" Ronald asked. "Why are you so invested in this map?"

"Surely I don't have to answer that," Malcolm replied. "Anything the Nazis are after should worry a lot of people. Whatever that map leads to should be lost to history. It's for that reason that you'll hand the map over to me."

"What you want me to do, Zane?"

I wanted to say, don't give it to him, but the coward in me forced me to say, "Hand it over to him."

"Nice and easy," Malcolm said, keeping his pistol tight against my forehead.

As Ronald passed the silver tube over, the General lurched forward. Shock filled his eyes, and he stared at me in disbelief before tumbling forward into the foliage, a knife sticking out of his back.

Carol stood only inches from me, eyes screwed tight, and she stared at me with wild tenacity. "He... he deserved that," she said. "He always loved my brother more than me, you see... he deserved what he got."

Moving to my feet, I reached out for her, and said in an even tone, "Carol, come with me. I can get you some help."

Carol backed away, her head swiveling back and forth in denial, and then to my surprise a thin smile graced her lips, and she said something very frightening, "We will meet again, Zane Carrington. When you least expect it, we will meet again."

Before I could reach out for her, she rushed into the jungle, disappearing through the thick brush and was gone. I regarded the General's body before turning to face Ronald and Lucas. Their expressions were ones of surprise and confusion, mirroring my own.

"What do we do now?" Lucas asked, baffled.

"We go back to the ship," I replied. "We still have a long trip ahead of us."

"Was all of this worth it?" Ronald asked.

I didn't have an answer. No matter what I said, my reply would sound hollow. As I reached out and took the silver tube from Ronald, all I could say was, "It's hard to tell what awaits us on the other end of this journey."

To find out what awaits Zane Carrington, read:
Captain Hawklin and the Ghost Army.
On sale now!

ABOUT THE AUTHOR

Charles F. Millhouse is an Award-Winning Author and Publisher. He published his first book in 1999, and he hasn't looked back. He has written over forty published works including novels and short stories. From the 1930's adventures of Captain Hawklin – through the gritty paranormal old west town of New Kingdom – to the far-off future in the Origin Trilogy. Charles' imagination is boundless. He breathes life into his characters, brings worlds alive and sends his readers on journeys they won't soon forget.

Charles lives in Southeastern, Ohio with his wife and two sons.

Visit stormgatepress.com for more details.

Printed in Great Britain
by Amazon